C000186950

About the /

John Steinberg spent many years in business before becoming
a writer in 2007. Since then, he has co-written and produced
comedies for the stage, published five novels, and has created a
series of books for children. *The Writer's Guide to Obscurity* is his
first illustrated book for adults. He is married with three children and
lives in North London.

By the same author

Shimon
Blue Skies over Berlin
Nadine
The Temple of Fortune
Three Days in Vienna

The Writer's Guide to Obscurity

by John Steinberg

First edition published 2023 by
2QT Publishing
Stockport, United Kingdom
www.2qt.co.uk
Copyright © 2023 John Steinberg

The right of John Steinberg to be identified as the author of this work
has been asserted by him in accordance with the Copyright, Designs
and Patents Act 1988. All rights reserved.

This book is sold subject to the condition that no part of this book is to
be reproduced, in any shape or form. Or by way of trade, stored in a
retrieval system or transmitted in any form or by any means, electronic,
mechanical, photocopying, recording, be lent, re-sold, hired out or
otherwise circulated in any form of binding or cover other than that
in which it is published and without a similar condition, including this
condition being imposed on the subsequent purchaser, without prior
permission of the copyright holder.

Cover concept and illustrations: Copyright 2022 © Fiona Wilson

Printed in Great Britain by IngramSparks UK

All characters and places in this book other than those clearly in the
public domain are fictitious, and any resemblance to real persons,
living or dead, or places is purely coincidental.

A CIP catalogue record for this book is available from the British Library

ISBN 978-1-914083-74-7

Dedicated to the Writer within.

As the saying goes, 'history is recorded by the victors'. This book is dedicated to another set of individuals: those writers whose success may not be measured by fame but instead by their resilience to keep on going, often in the face of adversity.

Norman, author of several works that until recently barely saw the light of day, knows only too well where you're coming from. Like you, perhaps, for a long while he just accepted the situation . . . until one day his curiosity got the better of him. Putting his latest novel on hold, he began to investigate whether there was any historic link to his own rather disheartening experience of what some might call 'underachievement'.

During his research and whilst re-tracing his ancestral steps, Norman discovered that he was descended from a dynasty of wordsmiths going back thousands of years, all of whom struggled at some time or other with many of the same trials and tribulations as himself. Yet somehow they had managed not only to survive, but also to pass down the lessons they had learned.

Norman now knew for certain that he had an obligation to follow in their footsteps.

This is Norman's story – and possibly the longest emergence from the shadows to illumination ever recorded.

THE NORMAN DYNASTY

ANCIENT NORMAN
4500 BCE

GRECIAN NORMAN
700 BCE

ROMAN NORMAN
700 BCE

DARK-AGES NORMAN
410 - 1066 CE

NORMAN NORMAN
1066 CE

MIDDLE-AGED NORMAN
1066 - 1600

EARLY-MODERN NORMAN
1600 - 1900

MODERN-DAY NORMAN
1900 = PRESENT

PART ONE
Ancient Norman 4500 BCE

Since time immemorial, man has found writing an uphill struggle so one might reasonably ask: why bother going to all that effort?

Yet one day it must have suddenly dawned on an enlightened individual that there had to be better ways to communicate than the traditional method of relying upon physical force to get one's point across. This individual was called Norman.

There was always a Norman in every generation who stood out from the rest, not just because he didn't have the same dress sense or lacked certain social skills; it was simply that he wasn't bothered by the normal concerns like trying to make ends meet and providing for his family. That was because he was motivated by something at a much higher level: an insatiable desire to create.

Frequently ostracised for appearing aloof was water off a duck's back as far as Norman was concerned. Being 'aloof' provided him with valuable solitude. You see, Norman was never lonely.

He had his thoughts for company, which held him in good stead for a while until four thousand years ago, when Ancient Norman suddenly acknowledged that what was missing was not a partner to share his life but rather an audience for his work, preferably one that wasn't intent on literally killing him at the first opportunity!

©FIONA WILSON

THE IMMEDIATE CHALLENGE FACING
ANCIENT NORMAN WAS HOW TO PERSUADE AN
OPENLY HOSTILE ENVIRONMENT TO ABANDON
ITS OLD WAYS AND COME OVER TO HIS
WAY OF THINKING, IN OTHER WORDS,
IT WAS TIME FOR
BRAWN TO GIVE WAY TO BRAINS.

Since there was no way that this transformation was going to occur overnight, Ancient Norman grasped that, in the meantime, those same limitations could be harnessed to good purpose. This was just as well since there was a whole range of obstacles that lay in the way of his early attempts to write. To start with, materials to write on such as parchment had to be sourced, at which point Ancient Norman required his neighbours to lend a hand, for he was well out of his comfort zone when faced with an animal carcass.

Then, before putting stylus to parchment came the tortuous process of making ink.

Attempts to burn wood or oil and mix it with water often ended with disastrous results as the liquid ran literally off the page! Glue had to be painstakingly extracted from the sap of pine trees to solve the problem.

And that was just the beginning. Ancient Norman also had to learn to chisel or paint signs on to stone surfaces or skins. Not being the most practical of individuals, he'd accepted help from those who didn't mind getting their hands dirty – although that help came at a price. For example, he might have to spend time choosing the right words for his neighbour to woo another in the community who had taken his fancy, but with whom he was having trouble making any headway.

Ancient Norman consequently found himself with an unexpected following of both sexes, all wanting to take advantage of his magical powers of eloquence and persuasion.

He was astonished when one of the ladies concerned identified Ancient Norman himself as the ideal catch! Before long, however, the unlucky woman discovered that not only would she always play second string to his writing, but that she would also have to support the family while her husband sat bent over his vellum, scratching out unintelligible words or tapping them out on a chunk of stone. Taking on the mantle of the breadwinner was something she certainly hadn't signed up for!

Norman now had a new mission: to learn how to communicate his literary works to the world outside his small community. To do this, he enrolled in fulltime education as a mature student.

Learning the skills of the trade

Becoming a scribe in Sumerian times was a long hard slog. Even for the elite for whom gaining an education was exclusively reserved, it was a challenge, and Ancient Norman soon discovered that he had taken on more than he could chew.

The Cuneiform script he was expected to learn by heart consisted of hundreds of characters and symbols. Nor were Egyptian hieroglyphs any easier. What's more, the teachers, consisting of former scribes and priests, believed in strict discipline. Students were literally whipped into shape for the smallest mistakes; none more so than Ancient Norman.

He had zero interest in mathematics, astronomy or the other subjects that made up the curriculum for the future priests and business administrators in their midst. For him, it was enough to put down on his tablet the stories that were stored in his head.

Falling short of the high standard required and considered a disruptive influence on the other students, Ancient Norman was frequently thrown out on his ear, and having to apply to his beleaguered spouse for the cost of the tuition at yet another school.

Jobs for the boys

Even when Ancient Norman had eventually graduated, his myths and poems were not selected for others to read. From this he soon learned the lesson that even if you were suitably qualified for the job, you didn't stand a chance if your face didn't fit. The secret, he decided, was to keep going, which was just as well considering what he was confronted by next.

Forced to go underground

Ancient Norman was one of the select few who possessed the skills to learn all the symbols and letters of their local language. These gifted people stood out in society as objects of awe or, as in Ancient Norman's case, suspicion. So when he started circulating his work privately, in the hope of gaining some readers and receiving some recognition, he had no idea that his talents left him vulnerable to the machinations of unscrupulous citizens. For instance, wily accountants on the take seeking a scapegoat for their own illicit activities, could use him to do the written work, and point the finger at him when challenged.

In the end, to avoid getting involved in situations fraught with risk, Ancient Norman was forced to uproot his family and flee to a safer environment like Egypt, where, if push came to shove, he could always find work training the locals to write on pyramids.

Making the hazardous trek on foot across deserts and high mountain passes, more disillusion followed when his new destination proved every bit as corrupt as the one before. Undaunted, Ancient Norman became more determined than ever to make his mark. However, once he'd managed to pass on his skills, Ancient Norman knew that his services would no longer be required and he'd then have to seek pastures new. Just as well that his pupils were slow learners so he could stay where he was for the time being . . . Until a completely new Hellenistic culture started to spread, courtesy of a young military commander named Alexander who renamed a city after himself! In Alexandria, Egyptian, Greek and Roman learning combined to create a powerhouse of culture and ideas.

Ancient Norman eventually set sail for Greece, full of hope that at long last his talents would find more expression beyond narrating religious texts and the exploits of Pharaohs of the past.

PART TWO
Norman in Ancient Greece c.700 BCE

By the time Ancient Norman popped up in Athens, with more than a spattering of Greek and Latin to his name, Grecian Norman could be forgiven for assuming that literary success was finally within his grasp.

It wasn't.

In the Greek Empire, a writer first had to get through the same stringent, character-building physical regime that was part and parcel of the development of the ordinary Athenian male. Those who, like Grecian Norman, were built more for comfort than for speed, had to quickly adopt evasive tactics in order to survive.

It wasn't all bad news. Literary works, particularly poetry, were transmitted orally, so being an old hand at the technique Grecian Norman wasn't backward in coming forward to take advantage of this new-found freedom of expression. Cornering passers-by, he would subject them to snatches of his speeches and poems. Although it was the custom to expect a reward for this, gratuities were rare.

This didn't matter too much to Grecian Norm because comedies and tragedies, performed in huge open-air theatres, were massively popular – and this gave him an opportunity to pen his own blockbuster of a tragedy. However, while writing this powerful drama, he still had to pay the rent and eat. A patron was required – which meant endearing himself to a wealthy man of influence who would be willing to supply food and lodging in return for having someone like Grecian Norman on hand to poke fun at politicians and government officials – something with which the patron himself could not afford to be directly associated.

There were other options too. If his playwriting didn't work out and he failed to impress, Grecian Norman could always gain back-door recognition by wangling a job as assistant to one of the famous playwrights such as a Sophocles or a Homer – especially if the work, in which he himself might have had some input, was entered into the main literary festival that took place in the spring in Athens in honour of Dionysus, the God of the Wine Harvest.

Competitions for the best theatrical performances were adjudicated by a panel of judges, and the playwright with the most votes was declared the winner. There was no shame in not coming first, since taking part was considered just as important as winning. If you had helped the contestant to get the award, you could rely on continued support from your patron . . . unless, of course, you were Grecian Norman. He soon found himself out of work again because he'd cast his lot in with a dramatist who had penned an irreverent diatribe against the gods and, as a result, had suffered their just retribution. Long experience had taught Grecian Norman to be adaptable, so he soon found employment with another orator, who had ended up in court and needed an appointee to enter his plea for him orally. At long last, as an early form of ghost-writer, Grecian Norman had found an audience and was even paid for his work!

Just as he had begun to enjoy some welcome stability, infighting amongst various parts of the empire let the door open for the powerful military forces of Rome to invade and conquer, absorbing the culture and marking the beginning of Roman domination in Greek history. Adaptable as ever, Grecian Norman made sure he was on hand to help with the literary side of things.

Norman in Ancient Rome c.700 BCE

Like his Grecian counterpart, Roman Norman was also involved in writing statements and other commissions for paying clients. Despite benefiting from the income and grateful for the opportunity to hear his own work being read aloud, he too had to be extremely careful. Ghost-writing could be a dangerous occupation, unless of course the client was an emperor. Then there was nothing to fear. Some rulers were eager to work with writers like Roman Norman.

Their motive was simple: to be able to show off their own works in a better light.

And it didn't stop there. Resourceful Roman Norman may well have had a hand in several Aesop-type fables that were only discovered much later. Perhaps the fable writer wasn't quite the literary genius he'd held himself out to be . . .

The adage of the time was obviously: What's the point of doing something if you can pay someone more accomplished to do it for you and then claim the credit for yourself?

Not all emperors were as liberal and ready to collaborate, nor quite the upholders of free speech they purported to be. Several were responsible for banning private events, where citizens gathered to watch satirical plays or listen to poetical recitals that their leaders deemed subversive. Some unfortunate writers saw their works being burned and their own lives hanging in the balance.

Despite their propensity for abject cruelty, the Romans were also a pragmatic lot. Aware that writers couldn't earn a living without being sponsored, they took full advantage of this. A hapless writer had to relinquish control over his writing and allow it to undergo strict inspection, especially if it was intended to be circulated in private amongst the city's elite.

A Roman patron expected to get his money's worth. In other words, it was very much quid pro quo: 'you scrub my back and I'll scrub yours!' For Roman Norman it was enough to be able to keep writing – even if it meant demeaning himself in the process.

PART THREE
Dark-Ages Norman 410 – 1066 CE

All good things come to an end, and so it was only a question of time before the Roman Empire disintegrated, with attacks by Germanic tribes to the north causing it to splinter into east and west. Norman had already thrown his lot in with a particular Roman General who, aware of his story-telling skills, wanted him to boost the morale of his troops during their journey to the island of Britain.

So far so good until Roman Norman's protector, fed up with the increase in the number of revolts, particularly those by a vengeful tribal queen named Boadicea, decided to up sticks and leave before he got booted out by the next people destined to rule Britain for the following six hundred years.

Abandoned in his new environment, in which Latin became the sole domain of the Church and the elite, Norman had to undertake a crash course in the local language. His transformation to Anglo-Saxon Norman complete, he found he liked the literature that accompanied it, such as the heroic tales of Beowulf. These were works he could relate to, since they had much in common with the virtuous poems of his earliest ancestors.

However, because they were relayed mainly by word of mouth, large sections of the work had to be memorised before they could be performed, a considerable undertaking. Fortunately, Anglo-Saxon Norman was quite used to the process.

More of a problem was how to make ends meet. Since education and schooling were under the sole jurisdiction of the Church, literature was restricted to religious texts. Anglo-Saxon Norman was forced to fall back on his ingenuity as a travelling entertainer, performing popular tales and poems to musical accompaniment; and more often than not throwing in some of his own compositions for good measure.

Norman Norman 1066 CE

Just as Anglo-Saxon Norman had managed to establish a niche for himself, he was confronted by yet more upheaval due to the invasion of a people who dwelled just the other side of the Channel. William of Normandy wasted no time in sailing across La Manche. When he reached the other side, he set about driving Anglo-Saxons back to Scandinavia and seizing the crown for himself. Norman Norman was sure that since his name showed a French heritage, it would endear him to the French-speaking ruling classes.

He was wrong.

TAKE **THE DOMESDAY BOOK**, ON WHICH HE ASSISTED.
ALTHOUGH THIS WAS HUSHED UP, THE COLLABORATION MAY NOT
HAVE GONE QUITE AS SMOOTHLY AS EVERYONE MADE OUT.
THE ENGLISH AND FRENCH COLLABORATION
WAS BY NO MEANS AN ENTENTE CORDIALE.

The biggest impact of the cultural invasion into Britain was the introduction of the narrative epic and romantic literature such as the legends of Charlemagne, King of the Franks. These heroic tales were originally performed in song form, which was a grave disadvantage to Norman Norman, who was tone deaf and couldn't sing.

Having to resort to the drudge work of writing religious manuscripts as the main source of his income, Norman Norman was frustrated by being unable to create his own stories. Daringly, he risked adding some of his own thoughts and ideas in the margins of the manuscripts, in the remote hope of being discovered.

But then he'd failed to learn from his ancestors' experience. It would take one of the more business-minded of his descendants to perceive that life would be a whole lot easier if he could find a wealthy backer for his various literary projects.

Middle-Ages Norman 1066 to c. 1600

As Middle-Ages Norman was to discover, sponsors were few and far between. Even a prominent author like Geoffrey Chaucer needed to have a day job or two to pay the bills.

Middle-Ages Norman was lucky in that being literate he could always find employment as a legal clerk of some kind. But then, using his genetically acquired Norman charm, he wooed and wed the daughter of a wealthy nobleman, thereby funding his career as a writer and having a ready-made audience for his work.

Mixing in the right circles put him in contact with some of the greatest writers of the day. When they wished to rediscover their classical roots, they turned to him for help. This was no big deal for Middle-Ages Norman, since he'd retained every scrap of the painfully acquired learning of his predecessors. As far as he was concerned, the works of ancient poets and storytellers were always accessible since they were recorded in his shared genetic memory.

Whilst his father-in-law's patronage was assured, Middle-Ages Norman used the time to try and get his own work performed. He had written a play and put his money into the theatrical production. Of course, his wasn't the only production around.

Competition between theatre impresarios was something Grecian Norman had already discovered hundreds of years before, when he tried transferring his Athenian play of *Odious Rex* to Sparta – and was given twenty-four hours to get out of town!

THIS TIME HE WAS MORE FORTUNATE SINCE HE'D **JOINED FORCES** WITH AN ALTOGETHER DIFFERENT LITERARY MASTER, **A PLAYWRIGHT AND ACTOR CALLED WILL** WHO HAD CLEARLY CAUGHT THE PUBLIC'S IMAGINATION.

WILL'S NOTION OF DRAMATISING THE CLASSICS WAS **MUSIC TO MIDDLE-AGES NORMAN'S EARS,** ESPECIALLY WITH TITLES LIKE JULIUS CAESAR AND ANTHONY & CLEOPATRA (WHOM ROMAN NORMAN CLAIMED TO HAVE KNOWN PERSONALLY!)

Longevity has always been an important feature of the Norman line. When first his father-in-law and then his wife predeceased him, their demise put an abrupt end to Middle-Ages Norman's comfortable home and financial support. The rarefied circles that he'd frequented immediately closed ranks against him and he was forced to reassess his future.

The arrival of print

Thanks to the inbuilt resilience with which he'd been blessed, Middle-Ages Norman was soon able to stand on his own two feet again. He was nothing if not an optimist.

Unfortunately, even though he had seen in print form a limited number of his own plays and those on which he'd collaborated, he was convinced that the format of printed literature was just a flash in the pan. It would never catch on.

And yet, if he'd delved into the past to the 'screw press' that had been used for wine and olive production in Roman Norman's time, he might have realised that the invention could be adapted for other purposes, such as printing. A similar process would now be utilised as an integral part of mechanisation, creating the early codex form of stitched manuscript or book – something for which Middle-Ages Norman was woefully unprepared.

Early-Modern Norman 1600 – 1900

The invention of the printing press was a nail in the coffin for those employed in the labour-intensive field of handwritten manuscripts – a skill that Early-Modern Norman had inherited from the myopic Middle-Ages Norman.

Along with a collective of the writers and copyists, editors, illustrators and bookbinders of the time, Early-Modern Norman now faced a challenge: adapt to the new technology or get laid off! Unlike his predecessor, he had recognised the huge potential of the printing press. The increased supply of reading material required a literate readership . . . and there was no one better qualified to help them get there than Early-Modern Norman himself!

The result of Early-Modern Norman's altruistic endeavours was that libraries sprang up, containing not just Bibles and religious texts but also a broad range of poetry, historical books and the very first novels.

Literature had begun to flourish. More advanced printing techniques led to a wider range of topics being published.

Within an increasingly literate population, some discovered a wish to become writers themselves! But there was one thing missing which the forward-thinking Early-Modern Norman was aware of before anyone else: namely, the need for an accessible record of words and meanings. Since compiling lists of words and meanings for their own use was a well-established practice of the Norman Dynasty, new words were merely added to what had already been recorded. Which was not much consolation when someone else – Dr Samuel Johnson – beat him to it! The most that Early-Modern Norman could hope for was an unacknowledged role in getting the 1755 lexicon produced.

All was not lost, however, because Early-Modern Norman's skills were very much in demand. No longer forced to rely on a patron for support, he could easily get a job on any one of the newspapers and magazines that were read by a middle class made wealthy through trade and industrialisation. These readers were desperate for political and business news that might have a bearing on their livelihoods. Journalism was a logical way for famous writers to supplement their income. Charles Dickens, for instance, wrote articles and short stories for the *Morning Chronicle*.

Early-Modern Norman went a stage further. He founded his own daily paper, the *Norman Times*, thus providing a platform for his own work as well as the poems and short stories that had been passed down from the previous generations of Normans. Unfortunately, he couldn't compete with the greater circulation of the *Morning Chronicle* and his paper was soon swallowed up by a larger concern. In what was possibly the first case of copyright infringement, Early-Modern Norm accepted a generous out-of-court settlement for his legal action against the new owners who had copied his style and content. Ironically, his work had received far wider recognition in the process than he could ever have achieved under his own steam!

PART FOUR
Modern-Day Norman 1900 – Present

During this period, education for every class of society raised literacy levels to an all-time high, and technology provided unparalleled access to the literary world. It was a time when quills gradually gave way to pens, and mechanical typewriters to word processors and computers. It should have been a golden period for the upwardly mobile Modern-Day Norm, but since he was an avowed technophobe, these developments presented just another challenge.

The period also gave rise to a new phenomenon: the literary agent, set up to pave the way (at a percentage) for his or her ever-hopeful authors to acquire fame and fortune.

Modern-Day Norman did not even try to be an independent writer but plumped for a stable career so that he could provide for his family rather than follow the hand-to-mouth existence of his forebears.

And yet . . . behind the busy façade of Modern-Day Norman lay an unfulfilled individual yet to discover the writer within – not that he knew where to look. Bearing in mind his rich genetic heritage, it was inevitable that he soon began retracing the same well-trodden path as his ancestors.

At least they knew they had talent. Modern-Day Norman had to establish the truth of that for himself. His unique Norman brand of humour might work, he thought one day – if he could find a use for it. Without leaving the day job, he tested the water by bringing out his own range of greetings cards, convinced he had a winner on his hands.

The business failed to take off, and Modern-Day Norman was forced to learn a lesson from those who'd gone before him: never to take his audience for granted – assuming it was ever there in the first place!

Now that putting pen to paper had become a daily routine, Modern-Day Norman soon forgot his initial disappointment and set about his next project: trying to get his three-line synopsis accepted by a major film or TV network. Aware that he needed a full-length script, he employed a past-his-prime theatre impresario who promised to turn his dream into reality. Unfortunately, and in the hope of reviving his own career, the fellow steered Modern-Day Norman's comedy in the direction of the London stage, rather than to the bright lights and big money of Hollywood. This was not at all what Modern-Day Norman had had in mind.

What's more, as playwright and producer, Modern-Day Norman was suddenly landed with the responsibility of finding a theatre to stage his work in, as well as employing the actors to bring it to life – and having to foot the bill for both. Early-Modern Norman could have told him that donning the producer's mantle only makes sense if the project is funded with other people's money.

When the production did not make the anticipated transfer to the West End of London or to Broadway, when losses exceeded the most pessimistic forecasts and sleepless nights spent counting empty theatre seats became the norm, Modern-Day Norman came to a decision: he would attempt to prove his credentials as a serious writer.

An introduction to a book publisher, open to new business, was a lucky break that gave him a lift and stopped his family from completely giving up on him.

Seeing his first draft returned with as many corrections as the original text, less resilient individuals than Modern-Day Norman might have thrown in the towel and gone back to the conventional nine-to-five existence. For him, however, former playwright and now aspiring novelist, it was merely the start of yet another process of learning on the only job for which he was destined.

The book launch and favourable press reviews, whilst encouraging, did not put him on the map or set the world alight. However, they did secure for him yet another change in representation and a revival of hope that a second novel would achieve the long-overdue success – a hope that was to prove as misplaced as those in whom he'd just entrusted his career.

Modern-Day Norman then decided to go it alone. Several more novels followed, creating as little impact as before except, once again, on his pocket. With an effortless decline in his fortunes not even equalled by his early predecessors who had started with nothing and ended up the same way, Modern-Day Norman's challenge now was how to keep writing and, in the meantime, find a way to survive.

And so it continued, until the years rolled by to the twenty-first century . . .

Today

Having done all his research, Norman had seen at first-hand how his predecessors, going all the way back to Ancient Norman and following the centuries up to Modern-Day Norman, had confronted almost identical ordeals to the ones he himself had had to face. The way forward was clear: it was his duty to share his experiences for the benefit of writers everywhere and for the generations of Normans to come.

He set about the task without delay.

It was then that, having accepted this responsibility, his fortunes suddenly changed in a most dramatic and unforeseen way. It happened like this:

ONE-FINGERED NORMAN

WAS JABBING CARELESSLY AWAY AT HIS LAPTOP

PUTTING THE FINISHING TOUCHES TO HIS MAGNUM OPUS,

CALLED **THE WRITER'S GUIDE TO OBSCURITY,**

WHEN SOMETHING EXTRAORDINARY OCCURRED.

NORMAN WENT VIRAL!

Norman could only think that he must have tapped the wrong button by mistake, since Amazon was showing that . . .

THE WRITER'S GUIDE TO OBSCURITY

. . . was selling like hot cakes!

Norman could scarcely take it in. Here, at long last, was the breakthrough – *and* when he least expected it! Perhaps that was because he hadn't appreciated, until now, the role that luck played. After all, how else would the Norman Dynasty have survived for him to have told the story of their struggles?